The Christmas Tree That Cried

Jane Garrett Marshall
Illustrations by Dean Tomasek

WRB Publishing
Palm City, FL 34990
wrb1174@comcast.net

ISBN-13: 978-0-9896247-0-1

Dedication

To my parents, James "Duckie" Garrett and Bessie Johnson Garrett, my sisters, Val and Anne, my husband Bob, my cousin Luther Garrett, his uncle, my Ferguson Avenue neighbor Mr. James E. Nicholson, the people of Hilton Village, past and present, especially all the children who attended Hilton Elementary School. To my hero Roy Rogers, his wife Dale Evans and all the Buckaroos, of yesteryear and today, who are inspired by two heroes to lead good lives as the Rogers family demonstrated in theirs.

Acknowledgements

I appreciate my cousin Luther B. Garrett, Jr. whose personal interest in the story led me to his uncle, Mr. James Nicholson, who vividly recalled the vandalism of the Hilton Elementary School tree.

My gratitude is extended to the Writer's Center, Bethesda, Maryland. There I met a sought-after memoir teacher, editor and coach, Sara Taber. It was she who first told me that my family stories needed to be published. Writer friends in her classes inspired me, especially Marie Garland and Peg Dwyier.

Author Elizabeth S. Trindal, *Mary Surratt – An American Tragedy*, taught by example, the significance of persistence and belief in the truth of one's story. Her support was most valuable. My sister Val G Mason shared her recollection; my younger sister Anne G. Fanelli, a retired reading teacher, reviewed rewrites ad nauseam.

The Florida Port St. Lucie Morningside Writers and a smaller group, Word Weavers, presented valuable critiques. Writers Leona Bodie and Diane DesRochers provided email line edits and offered updated critiques during their visits to my Tennessee home.

My appreciation is extended to my supportive friends in the Nashville Branch National League of American Pen Women and Hendersonville Newcomers Club Newsletter Editor Marty Crawford. I learned from Elizabeth Ellis's storytelling workshops to apply her story boarding techniques for telling to writing. And, her award-winning book *From Plot to Narrative* prompted me to comb manuscript pages for details.

Two other books are heavily highlighted, Deena Metzger *Writing for Your Life* and Tristine Rainer *Your Life As Story*. Meeting Ms. Deena Metzger at the National Storytelling Network 2012 Conference and later attending her workshop was an eventful experience. In a three-minute phone conversation about this book, Ms. Metzger zeroed in on a critical perspective, which with all the critiques and my own re-reads and re-writes I'd not thought of. Such is the value of fresh eyes. My heartfelt thanks to her.

I am blessed to have discovered Nashville artist Dean Tomasek. His delightful illustrations engage children in the reading and transport adults back to their childhood.

My cousin Gabby Pratt, the first in our family to publish a book, inspired me. My niece, Beth Mason Nease, an athlete and a nurse educator, has published articles, poems and a technical book. Their examples motivated me to publish my work.

Throughout my life people have appeared whose lives interfaced with mine in unexpected and mystical ways. I still sense the presence; see the gentle kindly face of my childhood minister Rev. Marion Brinson. As a child, I did not anticipate that my Junior Choir Director, Nancy Prillaman, would become, later in life, a close friend, and one I'd fondly call my spiritual mentor. Her wisdom words guide and nurture my soul. It was she who led me to our Disciples of Christ minister Dr. Fred B. Craddock whose workshops, books and CDs have enriched my life and enhanced my storytelling and writing skills.

I'm most grateful to Dr. Michael E. Williams, Senior Pastor, West End Methodist Church, Nashville, a notable, sought-after storyteller, speaker and a prolific biblical interpretative writer. His open-mindness re-enforced my appreciation and respect for people of different faiths I first learned, as a child, from my father.

In Hendersonville, Tennessee a seemingly unlikely person, a quadriplegic, rolled into my life at a Toastmaster's meeting. James Perdue, a star high school athlete with a baseball college scholarship now wheelchair bound, published his story, *One More Play,* and inspired me to finish books I'd started.

I am most grateful to Roy Rogers and his wife Dale Evans for the uplifting examples of faith exemplified in their professional ethics and personal integrity. The couple played an important role in my childhood Hilton Village life. A picture of life at the time this story took place would not be complete without acknowledging my love for the singing cowboy Roy Rogers. My heartfelt thanks to their son, Roy "Dusty" Rogers, Jr., for his permission to use a quote from his mother, Dale Evans Rogers, and for providing me with pictures of his parents for this book. I hope the time will come when children, once again, are fortunate to have heroes whose lives serve as models of honor and grace.

Even with all the support from those named and those unidentified, this book would not have been completed without the compassionate understanding of the most endearing man, my Teddy Bear husband, Bob Marshall. He understood when we married that he was second place to my childhood hero, a cowboy, Roy Rogers.

O CHRISTMAS TREE

O Christmas Tree, O Christmas Tree,
How lovely are your branches!
O Christmas Tree, O Christmas tree
How lovely are your branches!
In beauty green will always grow
Through summer sun and winter snow.
O Christmas tree, O Christmas tree,
How lovely are your branches!

O Christmas Tree, O Christmas tree,
You are the tree most loved!
O Christmas Tree, O Christmas tree,
You are the tree most loved!
How often you give us delight
In brightly shining Christmas light!
O Christmas Tree, O Christmas tree,
You are the tree most loved!

O Christmas Tree, O Christmas tree,
Your beauty green will teach me
O Christmas Tree, O Christmas tree,
Your beauty green will teach me
That hope and love will ever be
The way to joy and peace for me.
O Christmas Tree, O Christmas tree,
Your beauty green will teach me.

The song is a German Folk Song known as *O Tannenbaum*. The first verse is traditional German, and sometimes attributed to August Zarnack, 1820. The second and third verses are by Ernst Gebhard Anschutz, 1824.

Source: http://hymnsandcarolsofchristmas.com

CONTENTS

Prologue

A village, a school and a tree. It all seemed so simple and life was just that – simple.

Village neighbors knew each other, borrowed sugar, spoke in passing and sent their children walking alone to Hilton Elementary School built in 1919. Shortly after the last bricks were in place a white cedar tree, was planted on the school grounds at the crest of a slope overlooking the James River. Like the little children inside the school, the destiny of the tree was unknown. No one then would have ever thought that the tree would become the legendary symbol of the village. How could a tree bond together the village and the school? It happened.

In 1936, a healthy-block-away-walk from the school, newly-weds moved into 200 Ferguson Avenue. James Nelson "Duckie" Garrett, a native Newport News businessman, had married a Portsmouth, Virginia nurse, Bessie Valeria Johnson. On their return from their honeymoon, Duckie first took into the house an ironing board purchased in Luray, Virginia. Then, he picked up his bride and carried her across the threshold of their new home. Forty-two years later, their daughter Jane said, "That purchase of an ironing board on my mother's honeymoon symbolized a woman's lot in life." Jane waited to marry until she was thirty-eight!

Bessie Johnson Garrett   James Duckie Nelson Garrett

Duckie forever said, Bessie is the "sweetest woman I've ever known," and she'd say about him, "He's so kind he'd give his last shirt away." On the elm-canopied-street the couple strolled hand-in-hand, exchanging winks and secret smiles. Like them, their neighbors were mostly young, married couples starting their lives together. In this cozy environment Bessie and Duckie welcomed into their lives three daughters -Val, Jane and Anne.

Daily, Duckie sang songs as he drove the only family car to his business, Garrett's Confectionary, located at 4108 Washington Avenue, across from the main entrance gate of the Newport News Shipbuilding and Dry-Dock Company. His store provided workingmen supplies, food and beverages. Duckie's daughters loved best his delicious milkshakes and colorful sugary coconut-flavored candy with pink, yellow and green stripes. A favorite treat was a glass car filled with tiny beady candy. But, what drew his customers was neither the treats nor, perhaps, the lunchtime meal – his delicious bean soup with ham and his hamburgers and hot dogs. His friendly, joking personality attracted even more customers than his renown Garrett's Delicious Hamburgers advertised, "to build strong men who build strong ships."

At home, Bessie managed the house and children, joined the Women's Club book group, served as the neighborhood nurse for feverish children, and administered liver shots to a nearby neighbor. Like other women, she rolled her baby to the A&P grocery store on Warwick Road (now Warwick Boulevard); like other women she parked her baby carriage in a line with the others against the storefront windows; like others she left her infant sleeping, and like others went into the store grocery shopping. No one gave a thought to the 1932 kidnapping of Charles Lindberg's son. After all, that had happened in New Jersey to a famous man, and the bad man was from Brooklyn across from New York City – a place known to have lawbreakers.

Famous people did come to Hilton Village. The Colony Inn on Main Street attracted wives of United States Presidents: Mrs. Herbert Hoover, Mrs. Franklin D. Roosevelt and Mrs. Woodrow Wilson. Other prestigious guests, with business and social connections in Newport News, also stayed in the inn. However, their presence went largely unnoticed and they didn't attract attention from would-be kidnappers. That was not even a thought.

Neighbors' eyes watched out for any minor accident - a child falling off a bike or a squabble between youngsters. Any stranger passing through would have been noticed. There was a cohesive feeling among these residents who valued their children, education and aspired to achieve themselves. No matter what their job titles were, villagers were just down-to-earth, ordinary, everyday folks.

***

World War II changed their feelings of security outside the village. In 1945 the Garretts' youngest, Anne, age one, remained home while her two older sisters, Val and Jane, seven and six, pulled their red wagon filled with rinsed-out cans to a once-vacant lot several long blocks from their home. In a short time the empty lot had become a massive tin mountain. The sight almost seemed comical, like the cartoon scenes, the two sisters saw on Saturdays at the Village Theater. Only children understood there was nothing funny about this heap.

Youngsters were told their soup and vegetable cans helped American soldiers. The cans would be transformed into something called war materials. It was hard to imagine guns and bullets being made from a soup can. Nonetheless, innocent children, eager to be supportive to something they didn't understand, dumped cans onto the heap every week.

This made them feel like their carting cans to the tin mountain was an important job. But they didn't know what war was, or who the evil people called Germans were, or where they lived in that place called "over there." Routinely, villagers heard and felt loud booms as planes from Langley Air Force Base flew over their homes, shaking treetops and shifting pictures on walls. Sometimes Jane squinted up into the bright sunlight at whizzing propellers in the sky. She wondered *are our soup cans in those planes?*

***

Downtown across from Garrett's Confectionary Store, the shipyard workforce labored to fill the demand for ships. The employment office had to hire additional workers. At the peak of the war, there were 30,000 shipyard employees. It was said that in about every three months a 33,000-ton ship was built. The strain of the war showed on the faces of the weary workers. Not even Duckie's humor gave the laboring workers the extra energy they sorely needed.

Like the shipyard men, Duckie worked extended hours during the war years. Keeping his store open to provide meals for men who worked around the clock building warships was his way to serve his country. It was difficult to find workers for the night shift, so like the shipyard men; he worked extra hours and sometimes slept in the high-back booths.

***

June 18, 1945. It was just another day or was it? News spread that General Dwight D. Eisenhower was addressing the joint session of Congress in the House of Representatives. The Supreme Court justices, the diplomatic corps and other dignitaries were seated. The galleries were packed to capacity. His address indicated that the war was coming to an end. If only Japan could be forced to surrender, the war would be over. He was optimistic that it would be soon. And, then soldiers would come home and the shipyard workers too could return home to a normal life. So, too could Duckie Garrett. The news brightened another day for Duckie that once again extended into the late night and early morning hour.

On that June night he began his after midnight routine: washing dishes, scrubbing the grill and cleaning the one rest room. He took pride in having an excellent reputation with the Newport News Health Department for having the cleanest restaurant rest room in the city. He set an example for respect of his women clerks: there was no foul language in his store and men knew his expectation that the rest room be left clean for the ladies.

And, so it was the late night of June 18th 1945 that Duckie closed his store knowing he'd return home to silence. He was alone at his store and knew he'd be alone at home with no one to talk with except the family dog Blackie.

Finished with chores, he went into his enclosed office, sank into his old oak office chair and placed paper with a carbon sheet into his typewriter. He missed Val and Jane. His sister Phoebe had invited his seven and six year old daughters to attend her Camp Walker summer camp for girls. She insisted on his daughters coming as her guests. Duckie, a pay my own way man, wanted to write her a check, but his sister refused to accept it. She remembered the brother who sent her money while she was in college and she knew he was having a difficult time ever since a fire had spread to his store. Finally, Duckie agreed to accept her gift.

Jane and Val were so excited and yet a little anxious, so were their parents. It would be their daughters' first time away from home. In June Bessie and Duckie drove the girls the one hundred eighty-three miles to Camp Walker in rural Aldie, Virginia. They grinned at one another as they watched their daughters jump with excitement. Nodding at one another they knew their decision was right. They thought *our daughters will be safe* and the girls thought *we'll be with Aunt Phoebe*. In Newport News, she owned the Wee Wisdom Kindergarten where they'd heard her tell great stories. They knew being with her would be lots of fun.

While Jane and Val were at camp, Bessie with their daughter Anne went to spend time with her mother and sister Lucy in Norfolk. Bessie loved her husband even more for understanding her need to be with her family.

Even though he was exhausted the thought of his home, without his wife and children, drew him to his typewriter. He blinked his eyes and began to peck away on the aged clunky keys.

***

December 1957. After a fire spread to his store a third time, Duckie Garrett, counted change one last time before he closed his store forever

Dear Val and Jane,

I have just closed the store and have just about finished my work for today, you know what time in the morning it is by that and I am so sleepy I can hardly hold my eyes open. But, I got to thinking about you and wondering how you were making out so, I thought I'd write you.

We called you or rather tried to call you today, but couldn't get the call through. We miss you a great deal, I imagine more than you realize but I want you to have a good time and enjoy every minute of the time you are away. You know little girls have so much to learn and such a short time to learn it in that they have to take advantage of every minute. One of the most important things to learn is how to make friends and to be a friend and you are in a good place to learn that now.

I don't know who misses you the most Anne or Blackie they both look like they are lost. Blackie keep coming to me and wagging his tail and Anne keeps asking where you are. I took Anne and Blackie around the block before I came to work and I had a time with Anne. I drove around the block and then to the corner and she wouldn't get out. I brought her to the house and when I looked she had slipped away and was back in the car. So, I had to back the car all the way back to the house and get Mother to hold her while I drove away. I certainly wish you had been there to help me, the way you always do.

We had a heavy rain today and I drove past Teddy's house and he had built a damn and had the water back up in the street so he could float his boat. He was having a real good time playing with some other boys.

You would have laughed today at dinner if you had been here. You know how I play with Anne to get her to eat. Well, I was trying to get her to eat some Ice Cream and cake and she dropped the cake on the floor. Blackie grabbed it and Anne tried to take it out of her mouth. Well, Mother got tickled and laughed until I really thought she was going to be tickled twisted. You remember how she teased me about saying, "tickled twisted". Don't you.

Well, Daddy has to go home and get some sleep so I will say goodnight.

Be Good.
Daddy

Letter finished, he pulled apart the carbon copy, addressed an envelope for Val and one for Jane, licked and sealed the envelopes. Then he picked up his hat and headed for the door with the letters in his hand. As he turned on his car lights, he could see a battleship in the faint shadows. He sighed thinking *I surely miss the girls but out in the country they won't hear war news or sirens at night. They can just be children.* The drive home seemed longer.

***

The Walker Camp two-week adventure ended with festivities. Children told stories about their favorite moments. Jane and Val returned home with lots of tales about their Aunt Phoebe and the camp. Jane reported that never before had she thought how wonderful her family toilet was. "Would you believe I had to walk, at night with a flashlight, to a stinky old building called an outhouse to pee? There was no handle to flush! You just sat on a seat and did whatever. It went down a hole onto the ground. It smelled awful! Walking at night even with a flashlight was spooky!" Her sister or another girl always went with her, but it was still scary. Her parents had lived in the country and visited relatives there after moving to a town. They grinned and laughed recalling some of their own experiences.

Jane did *not* report on her sneaky tactic. During the day, she looked around to be sure no one saw her, especially her Aunt Phoebe or the camp counselor. Then, coast clear, she darted into her Aunt Phoebe's private bedroom near the front door. There was her aunt's secret bathroom, which no one was supposed to know was there. If discovered, it was off-limits! But, Jane knew about the sacred in-door toilet. She learned to pee fast and dart back out of Aunt Phoebe's room before anyone saw her. At night, she had no choice but to take the flashlight and venture out into the night with another girl and her secret star friend to protect her.

***

Hilton Elementary School 3rd Grade 1947
Jane Garrett 1st row last person on right

Home again, Jane walked past her school tree down the slope to the Hilton Pier. She knew school would soon start. There would be summer stories to tell and new things to learn. She heard that Mrs. Pierce, her third grade teacher, was very nice. That made the thought of school better.

Most of all, she looked forward to the new Roy Rogers movie coming to the Village Theater. Her Rogers' comic books were tattered from re-reads. At camp, she saved much of her twenty-five cents spending money at the country store for a treat she loved more – Roy Rogers comics. She couldn't wait to get to Rose's Five and Dime store to buy the latest one.

**

School started and the war continued. The threat of that distant country Germany didn't affect the villagers' personal sense of security. During the day, front doors were seldom locked nor were they locked at night. One late night, as was Duckie's routine, he once again drove home in the early morning hour exhausted. Unknowingly, he drove past his home, and continued across Main Street and on down Ferguson to the house located next to the end of the street – positioned in the same location as his own house. He parked the car, and no doubt, beyond exhaustion, said, as he always did when tired, "Woe is me." He walked up to the house, opened the front door and stood staring at furniture that was *not* his. Jolted, he realized he was in the wrong house!

Quietly, he tiptoed out, dashed to his car and drove around the block back to his own house. Late that morning when he awakened, he told Bessie what happened and concluded his story saying, "I could have been shot for being a burglar!" Bessie laughed; she knew there was no danger. After all, housebreakers never came to the village; they roamed elsewhere.

People felt safe, except at night, when sometimes shrill sirens signaled a possible sightings of an enemy plane. Villagers didn't talk about guns, or even, as far as Jane knew, no one owned one, except her father. He had one at home in his top chest handkerchief drawer. He said, "Never touch Daddy's gun. It's for my store, in case some bad man tries to rob me." But, it was always at home, not his store! Jane figured, if a robber appeared at her father's store, he'd just talk and talk and talk, cracking jokes with the would-be thief. Jane imagined her Daddy taking the would-be robber off-guard.

Her father would say, "Hey, brother, have a coke and let me tell you something." And, before the would-be-thief had a chance to speak, her father would jabber, "Once my brother-in-law Pop, and some men in a store where they worked, got fed up with a co-worker. Every morning the man took the daily newspaper and disappeared into the only bathroom. The man spent hours on "the throne" reading the newspaper.

Men waiting for the bathroom decided to take action. They got a firecracker, hid it behind the toilet and pulled the wire through a hole out the door. The firecracker and the wire were both well hidden. The next morning the man, with the newspaper tucked under his arm, disappeared into the bathroom. After about five minutes a match was struck. The men chuckled as the spark crackled on its way to its destination. Suddenly, there was a loud BOOM. The man ran out with his trousers around his ankle and his underwear under his knees. Never again did that man monopolize the only bathroom."

Jane pictured her Daddy hugging the shoulders of the would-be-robber laughing. She imagined the not-to-be-robber talking with her Daddy. The two, now befriended, would shake hands and the not-to-be-robber would leave chuckling with a hamburger and a coke. And, maybe, a part-time job.

Never did Jane see her father hold his gun. And, she never worried about her father being robbed. Over time, she came to realize her father's weapon was his humor. The gun remained peacefully resting in the handkerchief drawer her whole life, but her Daddy was always armed!

***

On December 31, 1946 relatives stopped by to visit with Bessie and Duckie. They sat in their small living room and turned up the volume on the Philco radio in the dining room as high as it would go. The war had dragged on and on for six long years. The radio was their lifeline. It was a habit to check in for the latest news report even when friends dropped in. Everyone was hopeful that the long war would end soon. A low voice on the radio was heard in the background.

"Shh!" Duckie said. "That's the voice of President Truman!" Suddenly the room had an eerie silence. The President said to a gathering of news reporters, "Gentlemen, I want to read you a proclamation…and when I get through reading that statement and proclamation…it will be handed to you. I have today issued a proclamation terminating the period of hostilities of World War II, as of 12 o'clock noon today, December 31st, 1946."

No one heard anything else he said or questions asked by the reporters. Everyone shouted, laughed and cried all at once. Over and over their voices rang out the news, "THE WAR IS OVER. THE WAR IS OVER." Jane and her sisters, mimicking the adults, ran down Ferguson Avenue exclaiming, "The war is over! The war is over!" Even though they didn't know what war was, they knew that everyone was happy that it was over.

Hilton families no longer heard, at odd night hours, a shrill siren that sent shivers over parents and fear into children. Immediately, when the siren blared, lights had been turned off and dark green shades pulled down. In the darkness there was no light – no light to enable enemy planes to target the shipyard or village homes. Wives no longer had to plan how to cook meals based on their allowance of war ration coupons. Sugar and other groceries became more readily available.

Years later, as an adult, Jane learned that her neighbor Mr. James Nicholson, who lived directly across the street, had often stood watch with a telescope on the roof of Hilton Elementary School; he was a lookout for enemy planes. Now, in 1946, the war was officially over; the shades came down, and volunteers like Mr. Nicholson stayed home at night with their families. Midnight shipyard shifts ended. And, Duckie Garrett closed his story early. His children sat on the curb anxiously waiting for the sight of his car. Like the country, the village once again returned to its normal routine.

Time that had passed slowly during the war years now passed quickly. Within the year, no one dwelt on the country's tragic past history – neither the 1932 Lindbergh kidnapping nor the fatalities of the long war. People throughout the nation were eager to move on and once again be happy.

The world was safe for democracy, and Hilton Village was far away from places riddled with crime – places like New York City and Chicago.

Normalcy returned. In the village enclave, protected like a fortress with a church on each of the four corners - the Baptist and Methodist on Warwick Road and the Episcopal and Presbyterian on River Road - men went to work whistling, women with adult sons in military service smiled. Children, who longed for summer and the chance to swim again in the river, lugged books to school. And every Fourth of July, youngsters, in homemade costumes of every description, pirates to Hula girls, waved the American flag as they pulled their decorated wagons down Main Street from Warwick Road to the Hilton Elementary School on River Road. Holiday celebrations, especially the Christmas tree lighting, drew the village to the grounds of the faded red brick school where the stately white cedar tree waited for its devout admirers. *This* was Hilton Village – a peaceful, church-going community. All was well, everyone thought.

But in this cozy place, an eight year-old child, Jane Garrett, faced a cruel reality Christmas 1947, and unexpectedly began a spiritual journey.

1. Christmas Overture

Before the last Thanksgiving turkey morsels disappeared, Hilton Village volunteers met at the sun-faded redbrick Hilton Elementary School. Old timers could tell tales about the school on River Road built in 1919. There, on hot, humid fall days, many a child had peered wistfully out the back classroom windows at the James River behind the un-air-conditioned school. However, that November of 1947 neighborhood men, women and children were not eager to swap school day yarns or summertime swimming and crabbing stories. On a slightly nippy Saturday, anxious children asked, "Are we going to decorate our tree today?"

Parents answered, "Well, it's about that time of year. Let's go take a look at the tree." Warmly dressed workers and hyper youngsters in zipped up jackets walked to the school to look at their beloved old white cedar.

Eyes scanned up and down the waving branches welcoming them. A man said, "Bet it's grown a foot or two. We might need more light strings. It must be ten-feet tall now." Another responded, "Let's check out all the light cords and bulbs before we go buying more." The adults went to the school basement and lugged out boxes marked with a red pen: School Tree Christmas Lights.

The daylong yearly tree-decorating tradition began. Folks from the 473 homes located on the six streets from the school on River Road to the businesses on Warwick Road came to assist with the decorating throughout the day. While some worked on the tree decorations, other neighbors brought treats from healthy apple slices to trays of home-made warm peanut butter cookies. Curious newcomers moseyed by to check out the tradition they'd heard about. In one way or another it seemed that the entire village was involved.

Children in lightweight jackets with colorful scarves helped to untangle the Christmas lights. Men in flannel shirts inspected the electric cords while women replaced burnt out bulbs. Keyed up youngsters carried the long strings of lights to men waiting on tall ladders. Throughout the day, giddy kids said, "These bulbs are really big! I can't wait to see them lit up!"

A man on a shaky ladder hollered, "Hey, Joe, hold it still, will ya?"

Joe chuckled, "You'd sure make a great tree decoration, if this ladder fell and left you hanging there."

The children giggled and laughed. It was fun to hear grownups make fun of each other. The teasing made the adults feel as though they too were carefree youngsters. A woman called out, "Treat time!" The aromas of hot cider and cookies welcomed workers. Youngsters dashed to the school steps and men stepped down off the ladders. Nudging one another a man said, "Looks mighty good." The frivolity made the annual tree decorating like a summer picnic. But, the big event, the nighttime celebration, was yet to come.

A mother called out to the children running around the school flagpole. "Hey, children come on over here. Let's see who remembers the words to the song we'll be singing Christmas Eve."

"Which one?" a boy asked.

"The one we sing to our tree."

"Oh," said a man in a deep voice, "let's all practice it now." With that he began singing *O Christmas tree. O Christmas tree, much pleasure doth thou bring me..."* Spirited workers joined in mumbling some of the words they remembered, while others nodded their heads, smiled and listened.

"We'll be working in the dark tonight, if we don't get these lights checked out," said the man.

"It's getting late," another volunteer worker added. "We'd better work fast."

"And, I need to get home," said a woman looking at her watch. "Come on youngsters, help us pack up the burnt out bulbs and move the empty boxes back to the basement storage room. Once again, the workers busied themselves testing the electrical switches that turned the light strings on and off at different times.

Everyone stood back, gazed at the cedar and smiled knowing their tree would look magnificent on the evening of their Christmas Eve Carol Fest.

" Christmas, my child, is love in action. Every time we love, every time we give, it's Christmas." Dale Evans Rogers

2. Night Before Christmas

Year-after-year, that's the way the folks of Hilton Village prepared for their annual Christmas Eve caroling. As always, a hum in the air persisted throughout the all-day tree decorating after Thanksgiving. Women worked at the school getting things ready for the program weeks away wondered *how am I going to cook dinner, feed the children and get my Christmas shopping done?* Somehow they did. The rush was also part of the tradition.

On Christmas Eve, after an early dinner, parents took their children back to the school grounds. They chatted, shifted their feet, and waited anxiously for the magical moment when the volunteer men rechecked electric light connections then flicked on the electric switch at the base of the tree. Even though the tree lights had been on before the carol fest it was on Christmas Eve that the village celebrated the official tree lighting. Gathered around the tree there was a sense of togetherness and excitement when the tree lights suddenly appeared in all their glory. Everyone knew that was the moment when the beloved Hilton school tree would wave its branches, laden with brightly gleaming yellow, blue, green, red bulbs. In its jolly way, the dazzlingly lit tree gestured a Merry Christmas to all those gathered. At this time, everyone joined in saluting the friendly tree, singing *O Christmas Tree.* Even though villagers knew the age-old routine, they simply had to be there for those cherished goose-bump moments.

Like other neighborhood children, the Garrett sisters scurried about their home helping their mother get ready for the holiday. There were presents to be wrapped and their tree had yet to be decorated. The family "rule" was that everyone in the family had to be present for the tree selection. With their father's late work hours that was not easy. It was not even a consideration that he, their playful Daddy, would not be there.

The night before Christmas Eve the family crowded into their car and headed for a tree lot. The selection was never easy. The girls loved tall trees with flowing branches. Those trees had plenty of room for all their bulbs, strings of tensile and more decorations, which they hoped Bessie would purchase. "Here's one," Anne said.

"Oh, my stars," Bessie said, "That tree is bigger than our house!"

Duckie chuckled, "Oh, Mommy, it's not *that* big."

Around the lot the family meandered pulling out one tree then another. After several possibilities were chosen, a final decision was made. "Let's get home," the weary mother begged. And, so it was that Christmas Eve day became a rushed time as everyone bustled about decorating the tree. On that busiest of holidays, boxes were carried down from the attic. The tree, transformed with lights and ornaments, became a living work of art. Then, emptied ornament and tree light boxes were lugged back upstairs to the attic. Except for carrying boxes downstairs and back upstairs, it was fun to the girls. But, to their mother it was another chore to orchestrate. "I don't know what I'd do what my girls," she'd say. "You all are so helpful to me." She moaned, "I've got to get this house cleaned. You know we'll have guests Christmas morning."

Bessie was determined that her home would be "company-ready." That meant the furniture would be dusted, the floors vacuumed, the windowpanes cleaned, the curtains washed, starched, ironed and the front porch, repainted in the summer, swept clean.

She told her children, "My mother taught me and my four sisters to take pride in our home." When her children acted lazy in picking up after themselves, she heard herself saying to her daughters as her mother said to her, "You're lucky to have a roof over your head."

Logical Val said, "But, mother, every house has a roof!"

Bessie sighed recognizing that her children didn't know or understand the struggle her mother had. She paused and with a tender look said, "Your Daddy is working hard to make sure we always have a nice home. Not all children have a home like ours. That's what is meant by "being lucky to have a roof over your head." We must show your Daddy we love our home." In this matter, she trained her three daughters, from birth, to have fun and to be responsible.

On rare occasions when Jane or Val moaned about picking up their toys or hanging up their clothes, she'd cast a *look* that sent shivers down their spines. She'd say with a hurt expression on her face, "Never in my life did I think I'd have thoughtless children who didn't pick up after themselves."

Jane learned not to respond in her haughty tone of voice, "Well, the baby sister Anne leaves her toys on the floor." That snide remark resulted in a *look* that would burn a hole in a twenty-one foot tree trunk of a Redwood Sierra. Every night the three picked up all their crayons, color books, wooden blocks and other toys and placed them in their toy drawer in their parents' bottom desk drawer. The radiant smile Bessie cast upon them made the few clean-up minutes worthwhile.

The sisters knew Bessie was their playmate and friend but foremost she was to be respected as their mother. People said in a gushing tone of voice, "Oh, you're Bessie Garrett's daughter!" It was a peculiar feeling to sense that it was like an honor to be her daughter. It made Jane aware that her mother, like her father, had special qualities that people admired. She dared not hurt the feelings of her highly regarded mother even when she didn't want to clean windows or hang laundry on the backyard clothesline. It was not until years later that her children discovered the meaning of her statement: "lucky to have a roof over your head." It really meant: lucky to have a father.

As an adult, Jane realized how clever her father was. He'd know his children were nearby, but pretended they were *not* within earshot. Her father would say to a relative or friend visiting, "Our girls know the right thing to do and do it. They help their mother and me when we need it. They're such good girls." His daughters made an effort to live up to his bragging compliments.

And, so it was in the Garrett household that Christmas was not just about selecting and decorating their tree or attending the school tree lighting or going to their church's Christmas Eve candlelight service. It was also a celebration of another tradition Bessie Johnson Garrett religiously honored - housecleaning. Her daughters liked better the tradition known as Santa Claus!

***

In the late afternoon, the phone rang at the store. Bessie said, "Duckie, are you on the way home? Remember the school tree lighting is tonight. The children really want you there with them." Then there was a pause. The three sisters exchanged glances. Bessie continued. "You're eating at your store? Well, all right. That would save time. We'll go ahead and eat early, and be ready when you arrive."

"Daddy's coming!" the sisters cheered. With renewed energy, the three finished picking up gift-wrapping paper, putting presents under the tree, helping their mother in the kitchen, and then placing their dinner plates on the table. No one knew or cared what they ate. Bessie didn't even bother to remind her daughters about table manners. Like her children, she felt a tingle of excitement, even though she was bushed. The anticipation of that magical moment when once again the school tree would light up gave her a quick adrenalin rush. So, she smiled and ignored the un-lady-like chomping and sputtering conversation with words spoken while food dangled between her girls' forks and their mouths.

***

Bessie sat nibbling her food. In the midst of her stress, she saw not her own three children, but herself at age seven, and her sisters Helen and Isabelle nine and five. Back then, in August 1916, the three sisters seemed destined to spend Christmas in the Raleigh, North Carolina Methodist Church Home for Children orphanage.

Her widowed mother had no means of support and her brother-in-law John urged her to place the three oldest in an orphanage. Confused and frightened, she talked with her Methodist minister who assured her that the Methodist orphanage, thirty-one miles away from her home in Littleton, would allow her to visit as often as she wished. She was tormented but believed the orphanage would provide better for her girls than she could. There they'd be well cared for, receive a good education and, most importantly to her, they'd be raised in their faith. She decided to sign Helen, Bessie and Isabelle into the orphanage believing she'd made the right decision, not for herself, but her daughters.

The day they rode the train to Raleigh, the girls thought it was a fun outing. Their suitcases were packed with clothes Mrs. Johnson made. She added crochet edgings to make their dresses even more attractive. It was, she thought, her last act of love.

At the recollection, Bessie shuttered. Her gabbling children didn't notice that their mother was far away in a different place, but Bessie was remembering another day, the day her widowed mother, Mary Green Johnson, had explained, as best she could, that the three would be together and she'd returned to the orphanage to visit them. They were too much in shock as the attendant led them away. It seemed their lives had been altered forever. At Christmas, Bessie saw herself, at Jane's age, in an orphanage. An attendant asked her, "What would you like for Christmas?" Bessie never forgot her answer. In tears she replied, "My mother." In an unexpected way, that wish came true.

Mrs. Johnson returned every day, wearing, as was the custom, her black mourning dress and long black veil. The girls, bursting into tears again, flew into their mother's open arms. But, then, two weeks later that August 1916, their lives changed once again.

The orphanage secretary took a risk. Before the girls arrived for Mrs. Johnson's daily visit, she leaned across her desk and whispered to the girls' mother, "Mrs. Johnson, the supervisor is away today. It will be your last chance to take your daughters home." Stunned, Mrs. Johnson sank down into her chair gripping the armrests wondering, *how can I support my three oldest and the two youngest visiting now with relatives?*

The secretary broke into her thoughts. "Mrs. Johnson," she said, "as much as you love your daughters, they'd be better off with you on bread and water than living here in an orphanage." At that point, both scared and resolved, yet not knowing how she'd manage, she spoke in a shaky whisper. "I'll take my daughters home."

Bessie held her table napkin up to wipe away a tear and shook her head. She listened to her children chatter about Santa Claus and smiled. She remembered her own childhood Christmas at home with her mother. Every year she and her four sisters received a pencil box with a pencil, an orange and a few pieces of candy. Sometimes she also received a book. After their two-week-stay in the orphanage, for the rest of their lives, the sisters knew the best Christmas gift of all was being with their mother and each other.

Lost in thought again, Bessie sighed. *My husband is not here, but he is coming home.* Her own father had come home from work one May spring day and died that night from pneumonia. She forever held in her heart the memory of her father's kind face and the little desk he had built for her. Determined that she, a nurse, would keep her family healthy Bessie gritted her teeth and silently vowed *my children will always have their father.*

"What's that?" Val asked. Her mother came out of her private world, blinked and grinned.

"Sounds like a car," she said. In her teasing voice, she added, "Wonder who it could be?"

"Daddy!" squealed Anne. Jane and Val jumped up from their chair and ran to open the door.

The three embraced their father who, as always, hid his fatigue from them. "My girls," he said with a twinkle in his eye. "Guess who is across the street?"

"Uncle Boozie!" Val cheered. The Garrett sisters knew their uncle had married their neighbor's daughter Virginia Nicholson, whose older sisters baby-sat for them. A visit from their Uncle Boozie was a treat.

***

Moments later the girls heard footsteps on the floor of their enclosed screened front porch. There was no need to knock. Uncle Boozie opened the door with gusto. Without an unnecessary "hello," he began, with a loud dramatic flare, the recitation: *"Twas the night before Christmas and all through the house not a creature was stirring,"* leaning over to wink at Anne. She drew in her shoulders, clapped her hands, and giggled, as he said, *"not even a mouse."*

Jane sat awe-struck. *This is Christmas.* Uncle Boozie came every year to recite the entire poem from memory. To her, this was just as important as the tree lighting tradition because *this* was *her Uncle Boozie.* None of her friends had a relative who could recite poetry by heart like her uncle and her Daddy.

After he finished the poem, the family applauded. Then Uncle Boozie and Daddy began reciting together another long poem, *Dangerous Dan McGrew.* The long story, told with a lot of expression, was about two men drinking liquor in a bar on a very cold winter night. Both liked the same woman, a lady known as Lou. The men got into a fight and one shot the other – killed him. Daddy said, "The story shows that drinking a lot of alcohol was a bad thing." Then Bessie with a sly smile said, "Lou wasn't a *real* lady."

The story took place in Alaska, which didn't make the poem scary to Jane and her sisters since there weren't bad men or bad ladies in Hilton Village. At least, none they'd ever heard about. Village people didn't even lock their doors. Those kinds of rough men and un-lady like women lived in big cities. She'd overheard her father mention cities with dangerous people -- places like New York and Chicago. Jane was glad awful things did not happen in Hilton Village.

Jane marveled at the ability of the two brothers to memorize such long poems. She'd struggled to learn the 100th Psalm in Miss Kitty's Sunday school class. That experience made her admire her father and uncle even more. From them and her mother, she learned to love poetry. Her mother read poems from *A Child's Garden of Verse* to her daughters again and again.

***

There was one poem she'd heard her father recite that she especially liked. It was about a tree. She wanted to learn it by heart, but she hadn't memorized it all – only the first phrase, *I think I shall never see a poem as lovely as a tree.*[1] She knew *that lovely tree,* for her*, was her* big weeping willow tree. There in her backyard she sat at its trunk beneath the slender flowing branches. That's where she hid and thought about important things: the boys who teased her about being chubby and the next Roy Rogers movie at the Village Theater. Alone, she read her worn Rogers comic books imaging she was riding alongside her cowboy hero. Beneath the waving branches of her weeping willow dancing in the breeze, she felt protected. But, on Christmas Eve she had to admit the loveliest tree was their white cedar tree at Hilton Elementary School.

***

Bessie said, "Boozie, we'll be going to the school Christmas Eve Song Fest. Would you like to join us?"

33

"Thanks, Bessie, but the Nicholsons are expecting me soon for their big turkey dinner. I'd best get back across the street. They'll be waiting. I know my nephew Jimmy will be at the school before long, though. He never misses the tree lighting festivities.

Val stood up, tossing her long brown hair "One more story, please," she said. The two brothers exchanged winks. Together they said, "I'll tell you a story of Jack McDory and now my story's begun. I'll tell you another of Jack and his son and now my story is done." The brothers laughed, the children squealed, and Bessie looked on with a peaceful but tired countenance. Boozie opened the door, turned and waved good-bye. His nieces jumped up and hugged him. "Come back soon," they pleaded as he walked out the door.

"Time to get ready to go," the girls' mother said. "We wouldn't want to miss being there when the tree lights come on." With that, the sisters scrambled upstairs for their warm jackets. With everyone bundled up for the chilly night air, the Garrett family started walking down Ferguson Avenue toward the nearby school a block away. The sisters began joyfully skipping down the pavement ahead of their slow-paced, handholding parents.

Bessie watched her girls, seeing herself, Helen and Isabelle skipping out of the orphanage to the waiting horse-drawn surrey. The clip-clop sound of the horses' hooves and the swish-swish of the white fringe dangling off the surrey's top cover had made that hot August day feel like Christmas. And, to the three not-to-be orphans, it had been.

Bessie turned her head and gazed into the eyes of her husband, squeezed his hand and smiled. She sighed to herself – *Christmas Eve. That's when my mother and father married.* She thought, *no matter what struggle Duckie and I might have, unlike my four sisters and me, my three children have their father, especially at Christmas.*

[1] Kilmer, Joyce. "Trees" in Poetry: A Magazine of Verse, V. 2, (Chicago: Modern Poetry Association, August 1913), 160.

3. Joyful Eve

The Garrett family arrived at the school greeting people who lived on different streets – Palen, Hurley, Piez, Hopkins and Post. While adults chatted, Val, Jane, and Anne ran around the school grounds with friends from their street and others who were in Val's and Jane's school classes. Brightly clad villagers with warm colorful red and green Christmas scarves wrapped around their necks waved and called to each other. Families stood and waited, conversing in whisper-like voices. Like the anxious anticipation of an appearance of a fairy with a magic wand, the mystical moment hung in the air. The onlookers waited breathlessly in the silent, velvety darkness for that wondrous split-second when lights would miraculously appear on the Christmas tree.

Then, a flick of a switch. A sudden brilliant mix of red, green, white and blue and the tree burst to life. A chorus of "ahs" permeated the air. The Christmas tree lights had been on for weeks but now Christmas was here and here in the village the spirit of Christmas rang though the villagers not their church bells.

Everyone cheered and applauded the tree and its lights. Voices of playful children and eager parents rang out, singing the traditional songs they'd sung for years. *"O, Christmas tree, O Christmas tree, Thy candles shine out brightly!"* Everyone loved to sing praises to the tree that brought them together. The children belted out the song *Santa Claus is coming to town* and *Jingle Bells.* Then to glorify the meaning of Christmas the mood shifted. The sweet sound of low voices began singing softly *Away in a Manager*. Village choir members began leading the reverent crowd in singing first verses of their favorite carols. As in years past, voices singing *Silent Night* reverberated ringing out into the starlit night journeying throughout the Milky Way, to find their place in the universe. Likewise, villagers too thought about their place as they sang *O Little Town of Bethlehem*. But, it was Christmas Eve and *Joy to the World* left them with a sense of contentment rather than puzzlement about who they were and what their place was in the universe.

In a somber mood the villagers started home chanting to each other, "Wish you a Merry Christmas." Excited children added, "Hope St. Nick is good to you!" As the evening ended, everyone wanted to scoop up all the mystical magic and hold onto those moments forever.

Walking homeward few recalled Christmas times in the not so distant past, when neighbors stood watch looking for enemy aircraft on the school roof. There was no threat now. The village was safe, everyone thought.

***

The Garretts waved good-bye to friends and headed home. Once they got there Duckie said, "It's time to leave for church. Let's all get into the car." As the car pulled away from the curb, he began softly singing, *It Came Upon A Midnight* Clear, instead of his usual *Home, Home on the Range.* He enjoyed singing that song for his cowgirl daughter Jane. She knew he rode a horse when he lived on his boyhood farm. Unlike her friend Roy Roger, he didn't catch outlaws. But, his store did sponsor a boy's baseball team, which he figured would help prevent their becoming outlaws.

Bessie, pleased to hear her family singing, closed her eyes and sighed, enjoying a few restful moments. She tried not to think about all the presents she had yet to wrap. The songs made the drive downtown to the 30th Street First Christian Church seem shorter, perhaps, too short for a tired mother.

The Christmas Eve service felt mysterious. In silence they walked into the glow of their church. The old wood pews felt warm as they slid into a long center pew in front of the altar. Candles in the windowsills cast a shimmering light against the darkened stained glass windows. The flickering light cast a mystical glimmer. Dimmed eyes, with no apparent body, peered through shadows. The soft flow of organ music made worshippers think about the Wise Men plodding along on their camels. Jane pictured the three gazing up periodically at a faraway star. She learned in Sunday school that it took the Wise Men a long time to find Bethlehem.

***

Years later, as a young woman, Jane figured out why: men don't stop and ask for directions. She pictured the Wise Men looping along on their camel arguing. "The point of the star is to the South." Another would say, "No, the angle is to the North." The third one, a wise man indeed, knew it was pointless to say anything at all. He just kept quiet and bobbed up and down on the camel's hump. The threesome plodded along forever. No doubt Jesus was walking and talking when they arrived. As an adult she discovered that it took the Wise Men, maybe two years or more, to reach Bethlehem. She knew the reason why. And, to this very day it is still true: men do not stop and ask for directions. She ponders *what was learned? And, did that expensive myrrh perfume evaporate?*

***

Jane always loved Rev. Marion Brinson, whose kind face and soft voice made her feel like he truly knew the spirit of God. On this night, he spoke about this, the holiest of nights. She thought she understood the words of the song they sang, *peace on earth good will toward men."* That was the feeling she had had standing around their school tree all decorated for Christmas. There was good will among the village people. The service ended with *Joy to the World*. And, then came more farewell greetings.

Even though Jane felt happy and content, the twenty-five minute drive home seemed too long. After all, it was Christmas Eve. Santa Claus! She couldn't wait to crawl into her bed, go to sleep and wake up too. In the late night, without much traffic, the car moved along homeward faster. The hum of the engine sounded like a lullaby. Jane didn't remember dozing off. It had been a wonderful day. All was well, she thought.

4. A Secret Friend

Jane heard faint voices. "We're home," said her two weary parents. The napping sisters stretched, yawned and crawled out of the car in front of their house, barely noticing their own brightly lit Christmas tree illuminating the street. They stood for a moment in front of their tree admiring its glow.

Anne yawned, "I hope Santa will like the cookies we made."

Duckie chuckled. "I'm sure he will."

At the mention of Santa Jane was fully awake. "I hope he brings me the *one thing* I really wanted."

With a twinkle in his eye, her father said, "What was that?"

"Oh, Daddy," she said in anxious tone of voice, "you know *what* it is! My cowgirl outfit! I need it to ride with Roy Rogers."

"Bet he went shopping in the very store where Roy buys his own duds." Jane stood up straight with her stringy hair about to curl up in her excitement. "Do you really think so, Daddy?"

"I never heard about a cowboy going shopping," said Val. "I thought they just hunted outlaws and chased cows."

In the dark no one saw Bessie snicker nor heard her say, under her breath, "Chase saloon joy girls!"

"Well," said Anne, "maybe they'd like to do something different. Daddy bought mother a present from a toy store."

Bessie nudged her husband and whispered under her breath. "You've really started something." The two exchanged glances and laughed. "It's a beautiful night," she said looking up into the sky. For a few moments the family looked up between the elm tree branches to admire the configuration of stars. "It reminds me of the first poem I ever learned. "Twinkle, twinkle little star, how I wonder what you are…"

Hearing footsteps, she stopped speaking, turned and looked. Down the sidewalk came two men carrying a very long saw. Each one held onto a wooden handle. The family stood and stared as they walked past their house. The saw seemed to extend the length of their car.

"Merry Christmas," Val said. The men said nothing and kept walking.

"Where are those men going?" Jane asked her father. "I've never seen such a saw."

He chuckled, "I don't know where're they're going, but it looks like somebody's gonna be surprised by a mighty fine saw this Christmas."

Val said, "It will be hard to wrap – that's for sure!" They all stared and shrugged at the men as they blended in the dark further down the street.

"Time for all of us to get to bed," Bessie said. "Yes," said Anne. "Santa Claus won't come until we're asleep." Val and Jane yawned agreement.

Their father opened the screened porch door and the family entered into their home through their unlocked front door. Up the stairs the children trudged. On this night their parents did not need to coax them to get to bed.

The three children looked like the images in the poem their uncle had recited. They too were snug in their beds nestled with visions…but not of sugarplums dancing in their heads. Their images were of SANTA landing on their very own rooftop!

On this night children everywhere knew a jolly old man with a long white beard, dressed in a bright red suit would come flying through the air on his sled pulled by prancing reindeer. Like other kids, the Garrett children placed a glass of milk and cookies in front of their fireplace. Jane silently hoped Santa would not get stuck in the chimney. She'd heard people say it could happen.

Jane snuggled her Teddy Bear close to her heart and then yanked the blanket up and over its raggedy brown fur. Her eyelids drooped. She struggled to hum the same carols she heard sung that evening at church and around the Hilton Elementary School's brightly lit tree. She loved all those Christmas songs.

Jane rubbed her eyes and then briefly wondered about the men she had seen that night. Even though she was tired, she played back the day's happenings in her head: decorating their family tree, hearing Uncle Boozie recite the Christmas poem, admiring the school tree lights, singing carols around the school tree, feeling the awe of the Christmas spirit at the church candlelight service, listening to the choir sing *Ave Maria* and hearing Rev. Brinson speak of good will toward men – even those you didn't like. That sounded hard. She shrugged and put questioning thoughts aside. Then promised herself she'd never forget all the joy she felt…all those tingly moments.

Again, she hugged her pillow and sighed. Like Christmas Eves past, she thought: *Wouldn't it be easier for Santa to land on rooftops, if we had snow? And, wouldn't it be a treat to live in places where children could sled all winter?* Jane faintly remembered the time it snowed when her father came home with a sled. Ever since then it leaned against shelving in her father's shed. She'd been told time and again…"it doesn't snow in eastern Virginia where we live." But, it did then. Sometimes she wished she lived someplace else.

She really wanted to stay awake and see Santa. Oh, she'd heard that Santa wasn't real, but why not? And, why couldn't it snow in Newport News? Hadn't she heard her father say, "Anything is possible."

She stared out the window. *Little star, where are you, my secret friend?* She turned, scanned the sky and spotted a flickering light. *Oh, little star, I wish I may, I wish I might have this wish I wish tonight.* She paused and crossed her fingers for good luck. *Please be sure Santa has my Roy Rogers cowgirl outfit on his sleigh and please let it snow.* She stopped for a minute and hugged her pillow tight. Then, she continued, *tell me why people should wish good will toward people they don't like – like the boys who tease me, especially the two who called me 'fatso.'*

More jumbled images floated through her mind as she thought about Santa on his way.

It was, as her minister said, "…a night of peace and good will toward men." *Nothing was out of the ordinary except, maybe, the two men with the long saw.* At that moment, she passed into dreamland.

5. Santa Delivers

"Jane, Jane, wake-up!" said her sister Val. "It's Christmas morning!" Jane turned over hugging her pillow. Sleepy-eyed, she mumbled, "Already?"

The sun was not yet up but the girls soon were. Jane stumbled out of her bedroom to stand yawning with her two sisters. Their parents shuffled from their room in their nightclothes and bathrobes. The family jostled at the top of the stairs. Her blurry-eyed father grinned, "Ready?"

The children echoed, "Ready!"

Down the stairs they ran, bumping into one another. "Santa came!" they shouted with delight as they reached the bottom step. In front of the fireplace was an empty glass and a plate with only a few crumbs. A note scrawled in large black letters said, "Thank you for the milk and cookies. You girls are special to your parents and me too. Santa."

Jane stared wide-eyed at the note. *Santa is real.* "Look," said Anne, "our Santa presents are all here!" She spotted right away a box that was long and narrow. "Whose name is on this?" she asked.

Her father leaned over and looked. "Hum," he said, "it says Anne."

Her face lit up as she ripped the paper off the box and opened the lid. "My cry-baby doll," she squealed in awe. Turning toward her mother, she tossed her uncombed brown curls and beamed. "Santa got my letter."

"He surely did," her mother replied with an impish grin.

Jane, like her younger sister, had written Santa a letter. After all, she reasoned, there was no need to take chances. Santa was very real in her mind. Bright-eyed, she said, "I hope my cowgirl outfit was on his sled. I need it to ride the range with Roy Rogers." Val and her father exchanged winks.

Anne, Val and Jane Garrett, Christmas c. 1947

At that moment Val jumped up from the present she was unwrapping. "Santa remembered! I wanted a baby doll I can feed. Here it is!"

She picked up her doll and cradled it in her arms. "I can give the doll water. It even wets its pants. I'm going to name it Jimmie after Daddy."

In silence Jane, the tomboy, cringed. *Why does she still like playing with baby dolls? I'd rather have a horse!* Jane stared at the doll. "It's a girl! Why call it a boy?"

Val said. "I can pretend. I want a boy."

Anne giggled. "What for?"

"Someday," Bessie said with her sweet smile, "you'll figure that out."

Jane spotted her name on a big present. "Oh, look! This has my name on it."

"Maybe," Anne said, "Santa brought you a cowgirl baby doll." Jane cringed but said nothing. "I sent him a letter." She wouldn't admit it but was nervous that Santa might have missed her letter and gotten her a doll too. That would be awful. She'd have to act happy. She fingered open the taped box, wrapped like the others, in Santa Claus paper. That was a good sign. She hesitated then opened the box lid. "Hooray!" Jane yelled. "Santa got me my cowgirl outfit." She lifted the clothes out of the box and hugged them.

Val looked puzzled. "You hug babies not clothes, Jane." But, Jane said nothing. Her younger sister Anne just giggled. "This is funny," she said to her mother who laughed too.

Just as puzzled as Jane was about her sisters' love for doll babies, her sisters didn't know why she didn't play with dolls anymore. And, they didn't understand why all she wanted to do was chase robbers with Roy Rogers through their father's rose garden. Of course, *he* wasn't really there, but to Jane Roy was *very* present.

Jane often talked her good-natured sisters into being the outlaws. Then, she, the chubby sister, whose stringy strawberry blonde hair hung limp beneath her cowgirl hat, chased them around the yard through the rose garden. Jane whirled her six-shooter cap pistol and shot up it up into the air shouting, "Bang! Bang! Stop or I'll shoot you." Like Roy Rogers, she didn't kill the outlaws, her sisters; she captured them with a lasso rope. Jane wasn't sure if that was a Roy Rogers rule or her parents. One thing was certain. There was no baby doll for Jane – only cowgirl stuff. And, even though her two sisters were not Buckaroos, they loved Roy Rogers' movies.

Jane held up her cowgirl blouse and skirt. "Now I'll look like a real cowgirl when I ride with Roy Rogers. He's the best cowboy ever. He sings and jokes around with his friends like Daddy.

Val, the lady-like pretend mother said, "How can you be a cowgirl without a horse?"

In a flash Bessie said, "Your bicycle will make a mighty fine horse."

Jane pretended she didn't hear her remark. With assurance she said "Someday Daddy will get me a horse. You'll see." Her father chuckled. Oftentimes he took his children to ride a pony and told them stories about his boyhood days when he rode his horse on his family's farm. Jane knew her father understood. Under her breath, she murmured, *"Someday."*

Jane's favorite book was *Billy and Blaze*. One morning Billy woke up and discovered a surprise – a horse in his front yard. Jane dreamed that, like Billy, she'd wake up to find a horse on her front lawn, so far, it hadn't happened, but she believed it would. In a low soft voice she said with conviction, "Someday, I'll have a horse and ride the range with Roy Rogers."

Her mother cocked her head, smiled, and thought *that cowboy will be long gone before we can afford a horse.* But she said nothing. She too understood dreams. She said, "Maybe someday, Jane, when you're older. You have plenty of time. You're only eight now."

"Look under the tree," Val said, "there are a lot more presents!" With that, the girls stepped over gift-wrap all over the rug and scrambled down onto the floor by the tree. Names were called and gifts handed out. Tissue paper flew. Crunchy paper muffled words of thanks. Everyone held up presents for all to see. Blackie sniffed her package, tore it open, picked up the doggie treat in her mouth and wagged her tail in thanks.

Then Jane heard a knock she never forgot – a frantic knock that signaled alarm.

6. Vandal Attack

"What was that, Duckie?" Bessie asked. "Is someone's knocking?" Startled, he turned and looked at the door. "Who'd come visiting so early on Christmas morning? It's not even eight o'clock."

Again, there was a knock only this time the sound was a firm BAM! BAM! Blackie barked back at the early-bird caller. The girls looked up from the mass of tissue paper and gift-wrap. Anne shuffled up from the mound and headed to the front door. "I'll see who it is!" She stepped over Blackie and flung open the door.

Chuck, a red-haired, freckled-faced neighbor boy hurried inside, sputtering, "Have you heard?"

"Heard what?" Val asked.

"The tree – our Christmas tree – somebody tried to cut it down!" The boy spoke so fast he almost choked on his words.

"Slow down, Chuck," Jane said. "What tree? Yours?"

"No, no," Chuck huffed, "the tree at Hilton School!"

"Not our school tree!" The girls looked at each another in disbelief.

In an anxious voice, Jane said, "I want to go see!"

"Me, too!" chimed in Val and Anne.

"First, get dressed," their father said, "You can't wear your pajamas!"

Jane grimaced, "Why not, Daddy? We'll have coats on!"

"Wait, Chuck," Val said, "Let's all go together."

The girls scrambled upstairs. In an instant they were back, dressed in play clothes, hurriedly putting on coats, scarves and gloves. Bessie reminded them, "You've got to get dressed up to leave for Norfolk by noon. You know your grandmother; Lucy, Doc, Isabelle and your cousins will be looking for us. Go on now, look and come right back. Don't stay long."

"Ok," they echoed. They all looked forward to their grandmother's hot rolls and coconut pies and they knew the ferry line for the crossing to Norfolk would be long.

"I can't wait to see Uncle Doc," Jane said. "Maybe he'll tell us a story about catching robbers. None of my friends have a policeman in their family."

"Come on, Jane," Val said. "You talk too much. We want to see the tree."

Out the door they all went. The children ran down Ferguson Avenue from their home at the end of the block to the corner at Main Street. There they stopped, panting, turned, and stared. They saw neighbors from Ferguson and families from Piez, Hurley, Palen, Hopkins and Post hurrying to the red faded brick school. No Christmas joy filled the air. Like soldiers, everybody walked at a fast march with stern prune-like faces.

Children didn't ask one another the usual question on their minds: What did Santa bring you? Adults didn't say, "*Merry Christmas.*" Puzzled children and adults alike wondered: *What's going on? Who would hurt our tree?*

7. The Tree Cries

Since the tree was planted in 1919, it had grown quite big and beautiful. But now the huge fifteen-foot tree tilted to one side with some of its strings of lights sagging onto the bare earth. Like the angry sounds of slashing hurricane waves of the James River beating against the Hilton Pier, villagers' voices rose in a crescendo. "Why would anyone do such an awful thing?"

As the children neared the school, they saw a truck with a sign – Tree Surgeon. "Do trees have doctors?" Anne asked.

"I never heard that before," Jane said, "but I guess they do."

"The tree is wobbly," Chuck observed.

Youngsters stood in the crowd. Except for a few muffled voices, there was a hushed silence. Jane recognized her neighbors, Mr. and Mrs. Plummer. The sisters squeezed in beside them. Anne whispered, "Mrs. Plummer, what does the doctor say?"

She took a deep breath and sighed. "The tree is hurt badly."

"It looks like it's crying," Jane said.

Mr. Plummer nodded, "That is the sap oozing from the trunk."

"Is it like the tree is bleeding?" asked Val.

"That's a good way to put it," he said, "The tree surgeon is trying to stop the sap from bleeding, as you put it, Val. See the bandage wrapped all around the trunk?"

They twisted their necks to see around people and saw the surgeon lovingly pat the tree. "That's about all I can do for now," he said.

"Is it going to live?" asked Chuck.

"Well," said the tree surgeon, "there's a good chance. Cedar trees are known to be good fighters. Your tree is twenty-eight years old. They can live a hundred years. We'll just have to wait and see if your tree has the will to live."

"How deep was the cut?" asked Mrs. Plummer.

"Oh, I guess it was about four inches. The trunk is maybe twenty inches. Some cedar tree trunks are three feet. The saw blade didn't cut through the center. That's good news too."

"Saw blade?" Jane cried out.

"Yes, the tree surgeon said, "there's no doubt the tree was cut by a strong saw blade. It was left here by the tree. I saw a man take it away. I know from the depth of the cut that an ordinary household blade couldn't have made such a deep slash. I'll be keeping a close check on this tree. It's a beauty."

Murmurs of thanks echoed in the gathered crowd. Waving good-bye, the tree surgeon drove off.

Mr. Plummer nodded. "It happened late last night after our community sing. There weren't any strangers here. Someone or ones must have been watching and waiting for us to all leave. Now, all we can do is say get well prayers for our tree."

Stunned, Jane stared into space. Suddenly she thought, *the men? The ones we saw last night? Should I tell someone about the men with the long saw we saw last night? But, I don't know what they looked like. It was so dark.* Villagers around her shook their heads. It was hard to believe such a thing happened. *What could I say?* Jane thought. *I don't want people asking me questions I don't know the answer to. Who were those men?* Again, she looked around. No policeman was there. She thought *I bet Uncle Doc would be here even on Christmas morning.* Then, she sighed. *Daddy will know the right thing to do.*

"Jane, Jane," Val was waving her hand, motioning to her, "It's time to go. We're expected for lunch at Aunt Lucy's. Remember? Grandmother called yesterday; she wants us there early."

Running to catch up with her sisters, Jane thought *Grandmother's! Uncle Doc will be there. He'll know how to catch the scoundrels.*

8. Daddy Counsels

Christmas chimes of the Episcopal, Presbyterian, Methodist and Baptist churches, on each of the four corners of the village, rang out hope. Healing blessings were in the hearts of villagers for their much-loved tree throughout that Christmas day.

Late in the evening, Jane crawled into her bed and stared again out the window. Her thoughts were not on her new cowgirl outfit or her desire for snow. There had been so much talking going on at Aunt Lucy and Uncle Doc's with Jane's mother and her four sisters and their families. Everyone in Mrs. Johnson's family wanted to be with *their* mother at Christmas to tell once again stories about their growing up. Their giggles and laughter drew all the children into the dining room to listen for a while before they left to play board games.

Jane had only a few moments with her father during the evening. Tired, he hugged her and said, "We'll talk later when there is not so much ruckus." So, she had fun being with all her cousins and aunts and uncles. She even dared herself to pinch a piece off the bottom of her grandmother's hot rolls without getting caught. The coconut pie was off limits. A missing sliver would surely be missed! The mischievous challenge made her forget, for a while, the school tree.

***

It had been a long day. She lay in her bed and squinted into the darkness beyond her window. *Oh, little star, where are you? Are you playing hide and seek with me? Oh, there you are!* Again she shared thoughts with her faraway secret friend. *Little star, I wonder about the men we saw last night. Were they the bad men who hurt our tree? Daddy said he'd call the police, but like he said, none of us really saw what they looked like or knew where they were headed. Uncle Doc said the police would have a*

59

hard time tracking down the men without more information. I'm sure the men we saw must be the cruel ones who hurt our tree.

She believed deep down in her heart that there was one person who could catch the bad men, but she knew people, including her father who best understood her feelings, would not take her seriously. She couldn't bear for her Daddy to simply pat her on her head in consolation, knowing he wasn't taking her conviction to heart. So, she kept quiet and simply whispered to her secret friend, *you and I know that the one person who could catch the bad men is Roy Rogers.*

The star twinkled at her. She hugged her pillow and smiled. *I knew you'd understand.* With that, Jane sighed and fell asleep.

****

The next day Jane watched her father, seated in his big brown reading chair, turn newspaper pages. The bad men were haunting Jane. She walked over and sat on the floor in front of her Daddy. Often her little sister Anne sat on the wide cushioned armrests while she, Val and neighborhood friends sat on the floor in front of him. Then he'd grin, and in a ceremonial manner, open the Sunday comics. He loved to watch the children squirm and titter in excited anticipation. He knew they loved to hear him speak in animation, especially the quacking sounds of Donald Duck.

However, that morning Jane wasn't interested in the "funnies" or hearing her father amuse her with his boyhood stories. She sat on the floor in front of him while he read. She whispered, "Daddy, how could anybody be so mean?"

He put the newspaper down in his lap and sat still for a moment, rubbing his thumb against his finger. Then, he said, "Human behavior is hard to understand. Sometimes people with hurt feelings will act out that hurt by hurting others."

In his tender manner, he leaned over and touched her head. "There are times, Jane, when unhappy people do bad things. Some men who come into my store have very little money after they pay their bills for food, electricity and rent. It hurts them to hear other men talk about buying nice gifts for their wives and children when they can't afford to give as much as others. They're not happy when Christmas comes."

"But, Daddy, how could destroying a beautiful tree, especially at Christmas, make those men feel better?"

"They haven't learned how to make themselves feel thankful for what they have. Except for the cost of the Sunday newspaper, it doesn't cost me anything to read the comics to you, your friends, and your sisters."

"And, everyone loves to hear you read and talk like Donald Duck."

He chuckled. "That makes me happy. Last year, Anne wanted a big dollhouse and I couldn't afford the expensive one in the toy store. I figured out how to build one with scrap wood."

Jane nodded. "Anne loves that dollhouse. I like playing with it sometimes."

He laughed. "When you aren't helping Roy Rogers chase robbers in my rose garden!"

"Oh, Daddy! So, maybe, those two mean men were unhappy because they wanted what they think we have. They don't know how many long hours you work even on weekends when other men are home."

"And, I miss you when I'm not here," he said.

"I miss you a lot. And, so do Val, Anne and mother."

He paused. "That makes our times together even more special."

Her father sighed, wondering how he could explain human behavior to his daughter. He continued, "Jane, being resentful of others because they have something you don't only makes yourself miserable – that's envy. Even when I was struggling to pay some bills, especially after a fire spread to my store, I found a way to help others. It gives me pleasure to make the men who come into my store laugh. That's all I can tell you – make others happy and you'll be happy too. That's the secret – help others."

He leaned over and hugged her shoulder with his hand. "Jane, we don't know the real reason why anyone would attempt to destroy our village tree. I know we're all upset, but the truth of the matter is that we should feel sorry for those men who did the bad deed."

"What?" Jane sat up straight and looked her father in the eye. "Feel *sorry* for *them*!"

"I know that's hard. Remember – they're unhappy. Just think about it sometime."

Stunned, Jane said nothing. Neither did he. Her talkative father sometimes knew the significance of silence. That was such a time. He watched his daughter anguish over his words then look up at him in awe.

He winked at her. "I know that's a tough thing to think about." He paused, lifted up his hand and turned his head. "Right now I think I hear some robbers in our backyard. Your pal Roy Rogers might need your help."

Her sad-eyed look faded. She brightened up. "You're right, Daddy! I know where those outlaws hide. Roy doesn't!" With that Jane jumped up, kissed her father on his forehead, grabbed her cowgirl hat and pistol hostler. She headed for the front door, then turned around and said in a reverent voice, "Thank you, Daddy."

9. Soul Search

That night when Jane looked out her bedroom window and saw the stars, her father's words came back to her: "Envy is bad." She yawned and promised herself she'd remember that the rest of her life.

Jane sighed and tilted her neck, struggling to see her secret star. She paused. *Oh, little star, so far away I have only one wish. I've always wished for snow at Christmas – even a day or two late. Now I want something else instead. Our school tree is very sick. Please nurse our tree well.* She paused. *And, help the police find the bad men.*

She tossed and turned plumping up the pillow under her head. Restless, she cradled her Teddy Bear close to her chest.

Gazing out the window she thought, *Maybe Daddy is right; maybe I should feel sorry for the mean men; maybe they were envious of the happy village families; maybe they don't even have families of their own.* But, she could not bring herself to feel sorry for those mean men. Maybe later, but not tonight while her lonely school tree cried.

Jane recalled her Christmas Day – opening presents, visiting her grandmother, aunts and uncles and cousins and playing with friends on her street. Yet her mind kept returning to the sight of her school tree tilted to one side. The tight bandages held together the trunk. She prayed the cut, like ones she'd had on her finger, would heal. She imagined the two mean men pulling the saw back and forth; cutting the tree trunk hoping it would fall. She wondered how anyone could be so hateful. No, she couldn't, as her father suggested, feel sorry for them even if they were unhappy men. They made everyone in the village feel miserable on Christmas Day.

Jane shivered and hugged her Teddy Bear again as tears streamed down her face. She looked up at the sky through her tears. The little star twinkled. "Oh, my! My star winked at me, or was that a kiss?" She pressed her nose into her pillow and fell asleep with one lingering thought – *while*

Santa was going down village chimneys, mean men made our school Christmas tree cry. That night so did she.

10. Through Darkness Joy

Months passed. Every day the school children studied the tree as they crossed River Road to the school. School bus riders cranked their heads toward the tree as they stepped off the bus. Teachers noticed heads turned and eyes focused on the tree. Going into the building, they stopped and stood to gaze at the bandaged trunk. At recess, they were sometimes seen gently touching the branches. The sick cedar heard whispered get-well wishes and felt soft pats on its trunk swathed in bandages.

Like others, Jane said, "I'm sorry. I wish we knew who those bad men were, but we don't. Please get well. Everyone loves you."

The newspaper didn't print the story about the crime against the tree or the tree surgeon's reports, but many villagers made daily walks down Main Street to visit their tree. They looked hard at the damaged trunk and checked the limp branches. They whispered kind words to the sick Christmas tree. Villagers wondered *would the sick Cedar be able to survive the bitter damp cold and raging windstorms?*

Alone at night, the tree moaned and groaned, as the frosty winds from the James River swirled through its branches. Its bandaged trunk ached with pain. The tree branches looked up into the night sky. One bright star in particular shed its light down through the tree to its trunk. It beamed a message: "You're going to make it, my friend. I see the children touching your branches and hear their voices and adults too praying for you to mend."

The tree moaned, "You do! I thought I was just a once-a-year Christmas toy."

The star winked at the cedar and disappeared into the Milky Way.

Left alone, the cedar made a decision. *Oh, my*, it thought to itself. *So many youngsters who play around me and adults who've decorated my branches really care about me. I see hopeful looks in their sad eyes.* The tree struggled to stretch it branches up into the sparkly sky. *My star friend, wherever you are, I thank you for your light. I will. I must live. But, oh, it hurts*

And, so it was that the tree fought back. The tree struggled to stand straighter and taller. Its trunk throbbed but every morning, as it looked down on the faces of encouraged children, the tree attempted to wave a branch. Only at night did it shed a few tears. It thought to itself I'll show those thugs the strength of the white cedar. *The children and the villagers care so much. I will heal.* The worst of the winter months passed. And still the tree stood.

***

By mid-March, youngsters and adults alike were murmuring to the tree. "Doc believes you've made it through the worst time, old friend. Hang in there." After the last whirling winter storm, neighbors once again made a pilgrimage to check on the Hilton tree, still standing tall. "You're showing these kids how to survive," said one World War II vet. "I'd march with you anywhere." He grinned, patted the trunk, saluted the tree and walked down the street whistling his thoughts *our tree is a good soldier.*

Week by week news passed through the village. "The tree branches are getting stronger. There are signs of new growth too. We have a miracle tree!"

***

Then, the day came when the school Principal, Miss Menin told the children, "The doctor says our tree is going to live. Your good wishes helped make it well."

Walking home from school Val clapped her hands, "Wasn't Miss Menin's news wonderful? Jane replied, "Anne, mother and daddy will be so happy." Together they ran down Ferguson Avenue into their house. "Mother," they chanted, "our tree is going to live!"

***

"That calls for a tea party!" Bessie beamed.

Anne whirled around in a circle singing "A party! We're gonna have a party!"

Jane laughed.

"What's funny?" Anne said.

"I was thinking. Maybe we should take the tree some cookies. Mother always says cookies make you feel better. Let's take cookies to our tree!"

"I doubt cookies would help the tree," Val said, "but the birds would like them."

"That's right, Val," Bessie said.

Anne sighed relief, "Let's give the birds bread and we'll eat the cookies." They agreed and sat down for their afternoon treat. The cookies disappeared.

Painting by Hilton Village artist Chee Klutt Ricketts

Garrett Home 200 Ferguson Street

11. Celebrate Life

Spring came. Dogwood trees bloomed, daffodils nodded and people smiled. The Christmas tree had made it through the winter. In the morning crisp air, the tree waved its branches up and down to the children walking up the sidewalk to the school. In one hand girls and boys jostled their lunch boxes and a book bags while motioning greetings to their old friend, the tree, with their other hand.

Miss Menin noticed the children and the tree saluting each other. She decided to plan a celebration in honor of their healed tree. Children made invitations and sent them to their parents, businesses and their special friend, the tree surgeon. In school, girls and boys excitely wrote stories and poems. Finally, the day came. Parents and children gathered in the school auditorium.

A boy stood and read his story. "I'll never forget the day our Christmas tree cried. Some bad people hurt our tree. Everyone was mad and sad. The tree doctor gave it medicine. Our class drew get-well cards and hung them on the tree. We didn't know if our tree would live, but it did. That's because we loved our tree well."

Then, the surgeon stood and walked up the steps onto the stage and beamed. "The tree will be here for many more years. Of all the trees I've treated, your tree was the sickest. It lived because you Hilton Village folks gave your Christmas tree hope and love." Then, he turned to the boy seated on the stage and nodded. "Young man," he said, "I believe you're right. You students and your parents loved your sick tree well."

***

Joy filled the air. Children in the choir sang. Soon all voices rang out *"O Christmas tree, O Christmas tree, much pleasure doth thou bring me!"* Jane imagined the cedar tree outside enjoyed hearing all the voices sing Christmas songs in its honor in the month of May.

Miss Menin thanked the tree surgeon, and then addressed the students. "Girls and boys, what can we do to protect our tree?"

Jane said, "My Uncle Doc is a policeman. He rides his motorcycle up and down streets to be sure people are safe. We should have a policeman watch over our tree, especially at Christmastime."

"That's a good idea," Miss Menin said. "The police station is nearby." Everyone nodded in agreement.

Someone called out, "Let's have a song." The school chorus began softly singing another version of the German folksong *O Tannenbaum*. The words seemed to meld into the hearts of villagers like warm gooey chocolate; they sang with robust joy, "O Christmas tree, O Christmas tree, you are the tree most loved…how often you give us delight, in brightly shining Christmas light! O, Christmas tree, O Christmas tree, you are the tree most loved."

Everyone smiled and nodded to one another. The chorus teacher invited the audience to join with the chorus to sing the last stanza. Joyful voices of praise sang, *"Oh, Christmas tree…your beauty green will teach me that hope and love will ever be the way to joy and peace for me, O Christmas tree, O Christmas tree, your beauty green will teach me."*

The celebration ended as people filing out of the Hilton Elementary School auditorium reached out to pat and hug each other. Words were exchanged, and a promise: "See you in November to hang the Christmas tree lights."

12. November Returns

Before long it was November again. As in years past, the Hilton School tree watched neighbors untangle boxed tree lights and heard men march with ladders. The tree grinned and waved its branches as if to say, "I like being dressed up."

One late afternoon, Jane and her sisters stood outside on the lawn. They paid attention to their father steadily climbing a ladder to decorate their own outdoor tree. Jane loved that tree – it was *her* very *first* Christmas tree. The tree and Jane had grown up together. Only the tree was much taller. Each year, more lights had to be purchased. It took all afternoon to put all the lights onto the tree. Sunlight faded into twilight. The sky looked dark and mysterious.

Her father shouted. "Ready, mother?" With that signal, she plugged the light cord into the electric outlet. Then, like magic, the tree suddenly glowed.

"Oh, Daddy!" the sisters cheered. "Our tree is beautiful!" Quietly, Bessie stepped down off the porch into the yard. She stood back, admired her family, and beamed. Her radiance matched the tree lights' glow. She knew that this Christmas would be especially joyous.

The Garrett family stood together, spellbound, in awe of their splendid Christmas tree with its many colors lighting up their yard. They didn't notice a car coming down their street closer and closer at the speed of a cat stalking a mouse. Anne, jumped and danced around the tree, then she suddenly stopped, shouting, "Look!"

They all whirled around and saw the car pass by their home. Val read the big words printed on the side doors- WARWICK COUNTY POLICE. They waved and watched the car as it drove to the end of their street. The car stopped at the intersection of Ferguson Avenue and Main Street. Then they noticed the flicker of the left turn signal. Cheers of joy rang out. "Yeah! The policeman is going to our school."

"That's good," Val said. "We want our tree protected."

Slowly the police car drove past the brightly lit school tree all ready for the traditional Christmas carol festivity. The officer smiled as he playfully flashed his car lights on and off signaling the tree a message – *"I'm here for you, friend."* In response the tree waved its branches up and down nodding, "Thank you.*"*

Jane stood for a while staring down the street. She recalled the previous year when she and her family saw the two men walk past their house. She shivered but wasn't cold. Thankful for the police, she thought, *"This year no saw will hurt our school tree!"*

Anne danced around their tree, touching its branches. Skipping in the glow of the lights, she sang, "I wrote Santa and his elf sent me a note. It said, 'Your blue bike is on Santa's sleigh.'"

"When did you get that note?" Jane asked.

"I found it under my pillow this morning and I'm keeping it *forever*."

In the evening dusk she didn't see her father and mother wink at one another.

***

In the past year, when Jane had passed by the school tree, she sometimes wondered again why the men had tried to destroy their cedar tree. Maybe it was like her father said. Maybe someone in the village spoke hurtful words to them or maybe they didn't have jobs, which made the men envious. She kept in mind her father's words: "Be kind to people – it makes them feel good and it doesn't cost you anything." *Then*, Jane thought *if more people showed care, like her Daddy does in his store, then maybe men wouldn't do bad things.*

There were times when Jane thought her father talked in riddles. He read a lot but his thought-provoking ideas did not come from the Sunday funnies. He told his daughters, "I left school when I was in the eighth grade. I was offered a job to manage a store. The job helped put my sister Phoebe through the Fredericksburg State College. And, I was able to help your Uncle Tootie the year he attended the Johnson Bible College. It made me feel good to help my sister and brother too. I wanted to go to college, but then I couldn't. I was working." Each time he ended his storytelling with, "Learn all you can in school and read good books." But, the books he read had few, if any, pictures. They didn't look like fun reading. He said, "My philosophy, psychology and religion books make you think new thoughts, help you to reason, and understand what makes people tick." But, they also made him say strange things.

***

That night Jane searched the night sky for her secret friend. She hesitated then swallowed. Her thoughts were like her father's riddle: *How could she at Christmastime be mean like the men? Why should she, like her father said, feel sorry for them?* Again, she thought about the words her Daddy had spoken the year before. In the months that passed she had kept in mind his advice: "Be kind to people." It was hard to be nice to the boys who called her "fat," but she discovered her father was right. She ignored their unkind words and acted like they didn't hurt her feelings. That seemed to hush them up. And, like her Daddy said, "It didn't cost her anything."

***

Many years later as an adult Jane remembered another thinking challenge her father presented. He always said, "You can do anything you make up your mind to achieve." On that dare, she completed, in her thirties, the Cappa Chell Modeling School program. Then, just for fun and the challenge, she went, along with the other students, teen-agers and one other adult model, to New York City for the Modeling Association of American International Convention. The teenagers said, "We're going to win a lot of trophies!" Jane and her adult friend Wandette winked at each other. "We're going to have fun."

Jane really laughed when she, a size eight from her teen-age size fourteen, heard her name announced three times at the formal awards banquet: 2nd Place Runner Up Photo, 2nd Place Runner Up TV Commercial, and Honorable Mention Make-Up. Amused, she thought to herself, *I might have won a runway-modeling trophy had the judges believed my age.*

Amused but frantic Jane ran to find her modeling school director, Miss Gladys Davis. The judges insisted she belonged in a younger class division. Miss Davis verified that her student Jane belonged in the Sophisticate division – not the class division for women in their *twenties*! Thrilled by the misconception, Jane was quite tempted to walk the runway in the younger division; however, she knew the truth would be discovered and the officials who erred might not consider it funny.

By the time Miss Davis spoke with the judges, the runaway competition had finished. At the banquet, she kissed her trophies and squeezed them tight: *here's to Daddy and all the boys who called me 'fatso!'* Loud and clear her Daddy's voice came through, "Pretty is as pretty does."

***

As a child, she learned at church and at home that Christmas was much more than the gifts beneath their tree. But, she hadn't expected to discover just how much more the Christmas message meant. Haunted by the sight of sap tears oozing out of the decorated tree, it was a lot for her eight year-old mind to think about that next year. She surely didn't, as her father suggested, feel sorry for the vandals. She wanted the bad men caught and punished. She resented their hurting the school tree; she remembered it cried. She tried to push the thoughts out of her head, but they kept creeping back. She couldn't quite find it in herself to have kind thoughts about the men who almost killed their tree and made the whole village unhappy.

As Christmas week drew closer, Jane struggled within herself. At night she squeezed her pillow, looked up into the sparkly sky, smiled at her confidante and took a deep breath. She knew what she should do, but could she? She stared out the window up into the sky for quite a while. Something kept nagging at her. Where had she heard or read those words, "feel sorry for them?" Then, she suddenly thought she remembered.

Very quietly she crawled out of her bed. She didn't want her sister Val, asleep in the twin mahogany bed across from her, to awaken. Jane tiptoed to the closet, opened the door and stooped down. On her knees, she bent over and reached to the back left side of the closet. There she hid special treasurers in an old green lunch box. Without making a sound, she lifted it out of the narrow doorframe and held it in her lap. Inside was a thin tissue-like sheet of paper – a letter from her Daddy written while she and Val were at Camp Walker that past August. She put the lunch box back into its hidden spot and placed old shoes on top and beside it.

With the letter in her hand, she crept out of the bedroom without making a sound like the tide moving at night, unsuspected, out from the shore. Into the family's only bathroom she tiptoed and turned on the light. Very quietly she put the toilet lid down, sat on the cover and carefully opened the fragile thin paper. Jane hunched over to read the letter; she squinted at the faint old typewriter ink. Puzzled, her eyes scanned the page searching for words. She kept thinking *what was it that Daddy wrote?*

***

Hilton Village, Va.,
August 8, 1947.

Dear Val And Jane:

Your daddy is a lonesome old man with the whole family gone and no one for me to talk to but Blackie and the livestock.[2] If they could answer back it would not be so bad.

All the children on the street keep asking when you are coming home. It seems as though we all miss you. Mother and Anne went to Norfolk to see Aunt Lucy and Jackie Thursday and I want to go over and get them Sunday if I have any help in the store.

I just can't make Blackie eat. I told her that you would be back in a short time and not to worry but she just wont eat. When Mother and Anne get home they may be able to get her to eat. I am going to get her a bone and some meat when I go home and see if she wont eat it.

I ate dinner last night at Aunt Helen's and I am going to eat there again to-night. Uncle Pop's Uncle from Florida will be there and they want *me* to meet him.

I got five nice large tomatoes out of the garden yesterday and we had right many in the house and I could not eat all of them so I took them to Aunt Helen. Confidentially speaking, because I would not want to hurt Mam-Ma's feeling, I think that the things in our garden are growing better than hers. But, she has more than we have and more different things.

Don't you worry about a thing *we* will take care of Blackie and the livestock until you get home and we want you to have a good time. I would tell you to be good girls but **I** know you will be good as you are always good but in your play there will always be differences of opinion, some may want to do one thing and one another and everyone cannot have their way all the time about what they want to do. So, you will have to give in and do things that others want to do and by entering into the right spirit you can have more fun than you can by doing what you want to do. But if you don't co-operate you will not be in a frame of mind *to* enjoy anything. Daddy had to learn that lesson in business and it is a hard lesson to learn it is what is known as becoming socially adjusted and you are getting so old that you will be placed in a position where you will have to make up your own mind about things from time to time, and you will have to decide **what** is right and what is wrong. You know Mother and Daddy cannot be with you all the time to tell you what to do and you are in a good place now to learn to do things for your-self, **and** do them right.

Daddy does't not pray for you to rich in money altho, it is nice to have but Daddy has found *from* experience that a bad turn in business or a bad investment will cause you to lose it. But, I do pray for you to be rich in character and to be able to live in accordance to the rules of society. If you are socially adjusted you will be able to play well with children and if you can play well now you will be able to live well when you are older. Don't condem children who do not play according to the rules. Feel sorry for them. Daddy

***

There, at the very end, was the answer. "…I do pray for you to be rich in character and to be able to live in accordance to the rules of society. If you are socially adjusted you will be able to live well when you are older. Don't condemn children who do not play according to the rules. Feel sorry for them, Daddy."

That's it she thought. The men who hurt our tree did not learn how to play according to the rules when they were children. And, now as grown-ups, they don't play well or obey the rules of law. Daddy says to feel sorry for them. *Maybe that's because they know people don't like them because they do not live, according to the rules*

Jane silenced her mind. In the stillness, she stared at that last paragraph. She thought again about his words, *"Daddy cannot be with you all the time to tell you what to do and you are in a good place now to learn to do things for your-self, and to do them right."* She sat up straight from her slumped over position, folded the letter and turned off the bathroom light. In the dark, she tiptoed back into her room and slid the letter underneath the dresser scarf. Then she crawled back into her bed yawning. She said to herself *tomorrow I'll put Daddy's letter back in my treasure box.*

Gazing out her window at her secret friend glowing far, far up into the sky, her father's words took on a new meaning. She recalled hearing Rev. Brinson say, "You don't have to be best friends or buddies with those you forgive, just forgive." Like her father, he too tended to speak in riddles. *Why forgive them, if you don't want to be friends?* A minister, she figured, was paid to say strange things.

Perplexed, Jane looked up into the galaxies and sure enough her secret friend sent her a silent message – a twinkle wink. She took a deep breath and slowly whispered, "I don't really understand why those two men were mean." Then she hesitated, bit her lip, thought about her father's letter and hugged her Teddy Bear tight. She stammered, "I feel sorry for them. Sorry that they didn't have a Daddy to teach them how to play and how to live with rules." She paused and recalled what her father told her months ago, "The men need to feel good about themselves." Then, Jane added, "I just hope those men make Christmas happy for others and their families too."

She knew she hadn't exactly said she'd forgiven them, but saying she wished that they'd make others have a happy Christmas was about as far as she'd venture. She took another deep breath. *Maybe,* she thought, *maybe that will be good enough. Maybe that's what Rev. Brinson meant about wishing everyone good will, even those who hurt you.*

With that said, she sighed, crawled under her bed sheet and pulled up the blankets under her chin. Like the warm coverlet, it was a comfort, to have a thinker Daddy and a puzzler minister. Even though each one posed perplexed thoughts, she felt at peace and content. In no time she dozed off believing that *this* Christmas would be the best one of all, even without snow, or a horse. It was enough to have new Roy Rogers's comic books. Her secret friend flickered back a goodnight kiss.

[2] Livestock refers to a rabbit, Easter chicks and Guinea pigs, Duckie gave his children.

13. Villagers Rejoice

Christmas Eve was merrier than years past. Villagers gathered again around the Hilton tree. The celebration of its survival was joyous. The tree looked more radiant with even more bulbs on its branches. As before, people greeted strangers and villagers alike. They all joined with great gusto singing to the tree, "We wish you a Merry Christmas." Villagers were surprised when the tree surgeon appeared. He looked up at the tree laden with strings of bright lights. "Couldn't miss seeing my friends," he said. People shook hands with him and thanked him over and over. "I'll never forget the lesson your tree taught me," he said.

"What's that?" Val asked.

"Your tree was loved well. That's what a Hilton Elementary School boy said last May. I believe that holds true for people, too. While treating your tree, I noticed the loving way Hilton Villagers regard each other. You folks have a Merry Christmas and a Loving New Year!" With that the tree surgeon waved good-bye, shaking hands with those nearby as he made his way to his car.

People stood silent for a moment. His words kissed the air. Someone began to softly sing, *"O, faithful pine, O faithful pine, you teach a goodly lesson, that faith and hope will never die, though clouds may cover all the sky, O faithful pine, O faithful pine, You teach a goodly lesson."* There was a moment of awed silence. Then yuletide well wishers extended the traditional good night greeting, "Have a Merry Christmas. Hope St. Nick is good to you." but that year and years thereafter neighbors added, "and, if you need anything give me a call."

***

Bessie and Duckie held hands as they walked down Ferguson humming carols. Ahead of them their children skipped and hopped, singing *Here Comes Santa Claus.* Bessie smiled and sighed. In her private thoughts she remembered the first Christmas without her father. She was only seven years old, yet, the memory stayed with her. She squeezed her husband's hand; her children's Christmas would be merry. And, hers too.

As in years past, they rode to their downtown church returning home half-asleep but excited. Santa would come. Anne's blue bike was on the way. Val and Jane knew their Santa had special gifts for them too. The three girls gazed at their empty stockings tacked to the mantle and then petted Blackie goodnight. Val reassured her, "You've been a good dog. Santa will bring you a big bone, I'm sure." Blackie wagged her tail and licked Val's hand. Jane came out of the kitchen with a plate of cookies. Placing them on the fireplace mantel, she grinned at her parents, "Remember the cookies are for *Santa*!"

"That's right," said Anne. "He'll need a treat after bringing in my heavy bicycle."

The girls kissed their parents goodnight and trudged upstairs, eager to get to bed.

"Sleep well," her parents called out as they headed into the kitchen.

After her sisters quieted down, Jane gazed out her bedroom window into the sparkly sky. She searched for her secret friend who sometimes seemed to hide. Tonight her friend seemed harder to spot.

Jane took a deep breath. *I guess my star friend figures I'll wish for snow again.* But, somehow this year snow didn't matter. Not even a horse. All she really cared about, all she really wished for was the safety of the school tree. She gazed again up into the galaxies. In the mass of stars one stood out. Jane gasped and thought *that's my secret friend.* Her star confidante winked at her and, with a mysterious twinkle. Jane smiled knowingly. Her wish came true.

Afterglow

The Hilton Elementary School tree lived and villagers, unexpectedly, learned through the vandals and the schoolboy a lesson. Words the boy spoke rang in the hearts of villagers. Like the school bell, his message rang clear: "Our tree was loved well." Those words reverberated in village life. Mothers sent their children with get well soup to those ill, and adults offered to help each other when needs arose. People made an extra effort to look after each other. People began to brag a bit about how they had helped heal the tree with their good wishes and tree trunk love pats.

The school tree listened to their words and felt grateful indeed for all their care. It thought *their kinds words did indeed help me heal.* Yet the tree felt a bit sad. Then, one spring day, when everyone was gathered on the school grounds celebrating May Day, the World War II veteran spoke up. "I know we're all proud of the way villagers, adults and children alike, helped nurse our tree well with all their kind words and gentle pats on its wounded trunk. But, I tell you, my friends our tree is a tough soldier. It had the pride, determination and commitment to fight back just as my outfit did in Germany. We can be proud of what we did for the tree; however, we should be proud of what our tree taught us."

At that moment, there was awed silence. The soldier suppressed his emotions and continued, "Let's all remember you lose only when you quit. Our tree fought back. It presented us with a gift, a lesson: be tough-minded and you will prevail. It didn't let those thugs win. We helped give our cedar resolve, but the tree made the decision to live.

He paused and choked. Adults shifted their feet and cast their eyes politely away from his tear-filled eyes. They knew he'd lost men in his outfit during the war. In a softer voice, he hesitated then said, "It wasn't going to die because our tree loves us too. Our cedar has given us a living gift that we've been singing for years – "a goodly lesson that love, faith and hope will never die." The soldier, with tears in his eyes, turned, raised his hand and snapped a salute to the tree. Then he quietly walked off to join his friends in the crowd. People nodded but couldn't speak.

A man broke the silence shouting, "Let's all give our tree a cheer – Hip, Hip, Hooray." And, so they did. Not surprisingly, villagers spontaneously added a loud, "We love you too!" Applause echoed down Main Street. The cedar lowered its branches in a bow of gratitude to the soldier.

The tree thought *the soldier understands. But, how could I give up when I saw the hopeful faces of the children? And, heard words of encouragement from the soldier and many other adults too? I believed I was just a once-a-year toy. I didn't know how much I was loved.* Then, the cedar slowly stretched itself up as tall as it could without pulling at its sore healing trunk. It waved its branches to all the villagers. Everyone was smiling, laughing, cheering, waving back and blowing kisses to the cedar. The tree thought *it's nice to have people for friends*

***

Jane walked around the school playground recalling her minister's riddles, to forgive even if you don't like the person and her father's counsel to feel sorry for those who don't play by the rules of society. She considered the outcome of following their advice and concluded her father was right. She remembered his words, "it didn't cost you anything." With a smug smile, she thought *Why not? After all, I am a Roy Rogers Buckaroo. And, I know the club rules.*

Throughout their childhood, never again did Val, Jane and Anne see the men with a long saw, and to their delight; never again did they see their Hilton Elementary School Christmas tree cry.

Author's Note

The *Christmas Tree That Cried* is based on an actual act of vandalism against the Christmas tree at my school, Hilton Elementary School, about 1947. My older sister Val G. Mason and I remember well the happening. Our younger sister, Anne G. Fanelli, age four at the time, doesn't recall the actual experience.

People have questioned me: what genre is the story? Who is your target audience? What is the story arc? Resolution?

Fairy tales or historical stories or personal memoirs are all stories that take you on a journey. A target audience means that the book is written for a specific age group. My heartfelt appreciation to all my friends in the arts, writers, storytellers, artists. I struggled with the limitation of this concept. Why stipulate that this book is suited for only children or young readers or adults?

Both children and adults need to have their minds and souls challenged to enter into a world that propels them forward into another time and place or takes them back to an event that occurred when they were younger and freer to explore ideas and experience magical wonders through words, art, music without required report writing and evaluations.

I am mindful of the numerous teacher in-service programs I attended when we, as teachers, were required to explore an activity as though we were a child or a teen-ager. We were questioned: what were your thought processes? What did you fear? And, what did you learn about yourself in that moment of time?

I've made no claim as to the genre. It is non-fiction and fiction. It is for children today and children through an age labeled senior citizen. It is set in a time period that, even though dates, styles and people change, is endless. It is what you bring to its pages.

***

The writing process has many twists and turns. The story tells you what it will tell. Writers learn the story has a mind of its own. Thus, many rewrites occur as the obedient author obeys the story muse. Such was the case when I, quite by accident, discovered two letters written by my father in 1945 and 1947. The letters said, "I will be in the story." I thought I was through, but the story voice said, "Rework the story. I'm in it!" I obeyed the command.

***

A story can be analyzed to its death. I listen again and again to the voice of Dr. Fred B. Craddock on his CD set, *On Preaching, Number 15: But What About Using Stories?* I hear him say,"…just tell it and leave it alone…let it stand there…give the listener (reader) something to do…if they get it, they get it…if not , so what?" And, I laughed, hearing him say, "Do you explain a joke?" And, if you do, he points out you take away the power and enjoyment of the joke. I heed the words of this highly revered minister and teacher. I explain not the story. It is what it is. I invite you to read and enjoy.

***

Appreciations are extended to those passed on. The redheaded boy in the story, Chuck Soter, and Mr. and Mrs. Plummer are no longer living to share their remembrances. I remember well each one of them that Christmas morning 1947 when I was eight-years-old.

The input of my cousin Luther B. Garrett was significant. He discovered his uncle, James "Jimmie" Nicholson, who lived across the street from the my family, remembered well the tree vandalism. In a telephone and later an in-person interview with me, Mr. Nicholson confirmed the truth of the story. He asked senior members of his St. Andrew's Episcopal Church, located across the street from the school tree, if they recollected the incident. Jack Dawson recalled how disturbed villagers were by the vicious act.

The validation of these two gentlemen confirmed the truthfulness of the story. I did not simply imagine this story. It happened. Life in Hilton Village will forever be held dear in the memories of those who sang carols around the beloved tree, especially those who saw our Christmas tree cry and passed their remembrances to their descendants.

After I first wrote the story from recollections, I researched the incident for further information. I requested an archival search from the City of Newport News Police Department. Mr. Lou Thurston, Public Information Officer, City of Newport News Police Department replied, "I find your Hilton story very interesting and I sincerely wish there was a way to recover any police report information on the incident. However, our records do not date back that far."

The newspaper offices of the *Daily Press* and *Times Herald* had no record of the incident in their archives. The author also requested through the Internet service, Ask-A-Librarian, City of Newport News Public Libraries for an archival search on the vandalism incident. Again, no information was discovered.

I thought that my childhood Hilton Library, now located on Main Street, would surely have a record or, perhaps, hand scrawled notes about the event. I spent an afternoon with archivist Mr. Gregg Grunow who pulled every imaginable file related to Hilton Village. Together we searched for any notation of the vandalism. Nothing surfaced.

However, to my surprise, Mr. Grunow discovered an article, "A Christmas Tree That Wouldn't Die," featured in *The Times-Herald*, Thursday, December 19, 1968. A second vandalism act had occurred. That attack was some twenty years later after the first strike. At the time of the second incident, I lived in Northern Virginia, where I taught in Fairfax County Public Schools. My parents, Bessie and James Duckie Garrett of 200 Ferguson Avenue were no longer Hilton Village residents – they lived in the Glendale neighborhood in Newport News.

It startled me when I discovered that there had been another attack against our school tree. That was another surprise I discovered while researching and writing.

I am aware that some folks will find it rather bizarre that all this time and effort in writing, researching and rewriting was spent on a story about a *tree. Or, is the story just about a tree?*

To villagers, the white cedar is more than a tree: it was and still is a unifier. It brings villagers together to a place where neighbors come to know one another, expressed care for each other, and gathered each December to sing carols. The beloved Hilton Village white cedar tree will forever be held dear in the hearts of those who sang carols around its stately lit branches. There the spirit of Christmas was celebrated.

You the reader decide, what does the story mean to you?

Epilogue

Cheers of MERRY CHRISTMAS rang out in the 1940s and still ring today when neighbors and friends of Hilton Village greet one another. Many have forgotten or never knew how the spirit of love saved the tree, which stands so humbly at a faded red brick elementary school. I still return home to feel the spirit of Hilton and to pay respect to the school tree.

In 2009, word spread through the village. The American Planning Association had designated Historic Hilton Village as one of the nation's "Top 10" Great Neighborhoods.

My sister s and I laughed. "No surprise! We always knew it was a "great" neighborhood." It concerned me that through the years, villagers might not know the story of the vandalized tree, or not believe it actually happened, if they'd heard it.

I wondered if people might think that the 1968 vandalism was the only incident that had occurred, since there was no police record or newspaper account of the earlier crime. It became apparent to me that the story did need to be written, and not just to record the wrongdoing. Villagers should know their legacy of care for the village and its people. The spirit of care and pride in the village is what makes it a great neighborhood. The story was written to honor Hilton Village, its people, its history, its spirit.

As for me, whenever I return to Newport News, the first place I visit is Hilton Village. It is always home to me. I routinely drive slowly down Ferguson Avenue and stop in front of my house. The gracious present-day owner has welcomed me in when I've knocked on the door. Once there, I feel again the presence of my family. Misty-eyed, I see childhood scenes replayed.

Afterwards, I drive to Hilton Elementary School, park my car on River Road in front of St. Andrews Episcopal Church, and walk across the street to the old cedar tree. There I stand admiring the legendary tree. I watch its branches rhythmically moving; I hear voices singing Christmas carols. I am home.

I speak to the tree. "My friend, you did your part to make this a "Great Neighborhood." The branches bobble up and down, waving a thank-you. I stand in silence, blow a kiss to the old weather-worn tree, wave good-bye and drive homeward to Tennessee. I cannot help but smile. In 2009, Family Circle named my community, Hendersonville, one of the best ten communities in the United States. No wonder I feel so much at home. I am!

ABOUT THE AUTHOR

Adventure is my name. My parents called me Jane Nelson Garrett.

Jane Garrett Marshall voices her values and concerns through print, grants awarded, and community service. An organizer, she co-founded a storytelling guild, led the re-organization of the state Tennessee storytellers, serves as the Coordinator, of the new state organization the Volunteer State Tellers, developed a storytelling program at a local public elementary school with special needs, chartered and led rebuilding of Toastmaster International clubs. This award-winning author, speaker and storyteller, holds degrees from James Madison University, The University of South Carolina and St. Thomas University.

Her story *Professor Up A Tree,* published summer 2004 in the *Montpelier* magazine, received the 2005 Grand Award for Feature Series Writing from the Council for Advancement and Support of Education awarded to James Madison University. Jane comes to writing after a successful teaching career, and the Virginia Middle Schools Association's *Crucial Link* published her four-part series on learning styles. She is married to a patriot and loves living in Hendersonville, Tennessee.

"If the story is beautiful, its beauty belongs to us all. If the story is not, the fault is mine alone who told it." Saying from the African story tradition.

Friends for Life. Michael E. Williams, Abingdon Press, Nashville, TN, 1989.

"I love the ending which is a lesson for all, and the drawings are excellent – descriptive and apropos for a story, which tugs at heartstrings!" author-artist/choreographer/performer, Doris "Joy" Thurston, integrates all her artistic senses: visions, paint, dance, theater into words, *Stroke! A Daughter's Story* and *A WAC Looks Back*, poems, *Oh, America! Memorial Poems to John F. Kennedy.* Her art works are in museums and private collections. Her religious dance, "Worship and the Arts," is in the permanent collection of the Dance Film Library in the Lincoln Center, New York City.

IN TRIBUTE

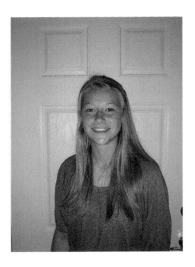

Amber Nease

July 8, 2011 my sixteen year-old great-niece, Amber Nease, died in a one-car accident when her car veered off the road and hit a tree. Amber was loved for her radiant personality and her acceptance of people regardless of culture, color or social status. She stood for her beliefs.

Amber had a never-quit determination to win, especially in sports. She played soccer, and served as the captain of her field hockey team. Even if there wasn't a chance the team could win in a hard-fought game, Amber would shout out to her players in the last seconds of the game, "Play to the end."

Her words are a legacy, especially for her Virginia family and friends, notably her teammates on her soccer and field hockey teams at Glen Allen High School, her Gayton Baptist Church mission trip friends, her fellow Bon Secours Hospital student volunteers, and her six first-cousins Kelsey, Garrett, Ben, Molly, Sam, Holly, aunts, uncles, great-aunts, great-uncles and grandparents.

In writing this book, there were times when I felt like putting it aside. In those moments of self-doubt, I'd hear an enthusiastic voice nudge me. "Aunt Jane, play to the end." In times when you too feel "stuck" on something, in a quiet moment, you might feel a presence and hear an encouraging voice whisper, "play to the end." Amber's spirit is with us. That I know.

Thanks, Amber.

The End.

CPSIA information can be obtained
at www.ICGtesting.com
Printed in the USA
LVIC04n2135160114
369809LV00007B/24

* 9 7 8 0 9 8 9 6 2 4 7 0 1 *